Pansys' village

WRITTEN BY LIDA KORDI

In terms of the language, God knows only one, and that is the language of love. If you are able to love his entity, you will be able to tell him what is necessary to be told. (Osho)

SCREENPLAY: Pansy s' village

SCRIPT WRITTEN by Lida Kordi

Publisher: Supreme Art

ISBN: 9781942912491

STYLE: Animation (2D, 3D) - Puppet theatre

Translated (Persian to English) by Mahin Eshghi & Parisa Moghadam

Typed by Masoomeh Jaberi & Zohreh Goodarzi

Photograph & cover design by Mehran Eshghi

E Book designed by Ayat Barari fard

lidakordi@yahoo.com

avayepeivandemelal@gmail.com

WWW.LIDAKORDI.COM

ABOUT SUBJECT OF STORY: The story is about different ways of animal persecute on in different area of the world in some countries:

Names of animals are used for insulting and abusiveness. Even they liken people's appearances and behaviors to animals.

*For keeping animals in the houses, people castrate them that so hurtful for animals.

*The Circus, zoo and some medical laboratories are three places where animals are abused and tormented.

*Holding some festival like bullfighting in Spain, Ully in China, Deopokhari in Nepal and…

*To abandon domestic animals at streets because of inability to keep or giving to the others.

The common proverbs that insult appearances or some features of animals like:

-A black hen lays a white egg. (The neighbor's hen is a goose)

-He is always crabbing. (He / She clucking like a hen)

-The hen has one foot.

THE CHARACTERS OF THE STORY:

(**Mr. Bull, Mrs. Cow, Calf**) which belong to Grocer and his wife Lady Gardener

(**He-ass, Foal**) which belong to Miller

(**Billy goat, Kid, Sheep, Lamb and 5 Pigeons**) which belong to greengrocer

 (**Mr. Pig, Mrs. Sow, 5 Piglets**) which belong to Two Brothers, the restaurateurs

(**Mr. Cock, Mrs. Hen, 3 Chicks, Turkey**) which belong to Priest

(**Mrs. Duck, 3 Ducklings**) which belong to Lady Tailor

(**Horse**) which belongs to Farmer

(**Miss Poop**) which belongs to Little Shepherd

Tomcat – **Female cat** –**Gold fish** – **Wild animals** (**Pelicans, Foxes, Elephants** … and **their Children**) – Head – Titi and Mimi (twin sister and brother) – Anti Riot police (police chief, police officer, policemen, policewomen) – Photographers, reporters and cameramen (ladies, gentlemen)

EXT.PANSYVILLAGE - DAY

<L S> Pansy village.

Pansy is a so beautiful village with some colored cottages, the church with a big bell, full of fences of box-tree. White roses, colorful violets, red trumpet-flowers have grown between them. White fences around yards of cottages.

Narrator:

>"Once upon a time, under blue sky, beautiful and
>
>green Pansy village had slept calmly. In this village
>
>many domestic animals lived beside the people;
>
>the useful animals that people couldn't live easily
>
>without them ;such as this rainbow Cock."

A Cock has stood at front of the door of the chicken coop. He is combing his amaranth, beard and tail. He is breaking an egg on his knees and then eating that's contains. He is clearing his throat. Then he is training his larynx with different sounds.

Cock:

>"A A A... E E E... O O O... I I I... U U U..."

The Cock is forming his beak to different shapes and chewing gum, unreal. He is moving his feathers and going towards to his unique place, in highest fence proudly.

<S> Cock on his foots is moving with gymnasium music harmoniously. He is jumping on high fence.

Cock (*flapping his wings and singing*)**:**

>"Doodle doo... doodle doo..."

Narrator:

>"This Cock was so systematic and regular, just the

other animals of Pansy and he did his duty well.

Every morning before rising of the sun he awakened

the people with singing. Pansy people so trusted

on the Cock even they didn't need their clocks."

Sequence 2:

INT.ROOMSOF COTTAGES - DAY

<S> Some damaged clocks.

- A clock with rusty springs out of head, like curly hair.
- A clock instead moving chick, there is a chick picture frame with a black ribbon in.
- A clock in a clown shape with spring out of pupil eye.
- A clock with two hands that closed by a swing from spider and small spiders are swinging.
- A clock without handle that dropped between baby`s toys...

Narrator:

"Let's go to meet to the other Pansy animals. Oh!

Here is so dark!"

Sequence 3:

INT. STABLE - DAY

The camera is pulling in the dark stable.

<C U> A pair of big and frightened eyes that stare at the camera.

<C U> A pair of eyes totally like those eyes but squint.

<C U> A pair of eyes like those eyes but childishly.

Narrator:

"Light ! Where is the light?"

The space is lighted a little.

<S>Two snouts full of grass. One of the snouts is big and another small. The space is more lighted. These scenes are seen:

- A huge bull that named Mr. Bull, practicing round Indian club and traditional sport.
- Mrs. Cow has put a vibrating belt on her waist.
- A thin Calf, is sucking his mother's milk.

Narrator:

"These cows belong to grocer. His wife Lady

Gardener grows the most beautiful flowers

in the world."

Sequence 4:

INT. FOLD - DAY

The camera is pulling in the fold.

Narrator:

"Here is Greengrocer's fold!"

<L S> The Billy-goat, the Kid, the Sheep and the Lamb.

Billy-goat is solving a sudoku puzzle. Sheep is spinning his wool by a spindle. Kid and Lamb are playing among straws.

Sequence 5:

INT. MILLER'S STABLE-DAY

<M S>Two big and small packsaddles are hanged on the wall of the stable. They belong to donkey and his Foal. Their names are He-ass and Foal.

Narrator:

"And this is Miller's donkey, too."

He-ass has installed a newspaper on the wall with nail and has stood opposite it. He is weight lifting to strengthen his arms just as he is reading the newspaper. Foal's toy is some gunny bags full of straws. He is trying to keep his balance with putting some bags on himself back. Every time when he adds one more bag with keeping his balance, he becomes happier.

Sequence 6:

INT. PRIEST'S CHICKEN COOPER - DAY

Narrator:

"Welcome to Pansy priest."

A turkey with installation a broken mirror on the wall of the chicken coop, made a dressing table for herself. Her name's Turkey. She has sat front of it and is making up. She has blue eye shadow on her eyelid. Sheis combing her feathers and rubs lipstick on her beak. On the other side of stable, a Hen is changing her three yellow Chicks wet diaper. Her name is Hen. One of Chicks is a girl; very fat and circular with pink cheek totally red beak and big, shy and black eyes with long eyelashes. Her name is Fat chick. She has taken her doll in her arm. Hen is arranging her flowered dress. One of two thin Chicks is trying to escape from pampering. Hen held him fast then changed two thin chick's diapers quickly. She is combing their forelocks. Then she is clearing the baby cradles. The cradles are made of egg shell. Hen is making up herself a little. She is combing her two tails, well and giving good shape carefully. She is paying attention to her tails deeply. Two thin Chicks saw a beetle and follow it. Fat Chick has assumed her doll with a ribbon.

The camera pulls in other chicken coop.

Sequence 7:

INT. LADY TAILOR'S CHICKEN COOP- DAY

Narrator:

"Be familiar with Lady Tailor's Duck and her cuddly

Ducklings. She is a Known tailor in this village."

Ms. Duck is arranging her three Chicks in a line and standing opposite the line like aerobic coach does warm-up and dynamic exercises. The forth chick has stood on her mother back. When Ducklings do balance exercises, one of them has a big belly and huge buttocks, suddenly hid crotch pants and his arm seam split. Duckling that has stood his behind laughs at him softly and slowly.

The camera is pulling in a dog house.

INT. DOG HOUSE - DAY

The house is empty.

Narrator:

>"Have you wondered about what, now? Did you expect to see a sleeping dog in dog house? No, You never will see such as this scene because (*the dog has worn army combat uniform <ACU> and she has a mace in her hand and a baton on her waist. She is guarding around. She jumps on the roof quickly and shades her hand on her eyes and sees far away.*)
>Miss. Poop is a dutiful and she belonged to little shepherd in the village."

INT. KITCHEN - DAY

The camera is pulling in a messy and dirty kitchen.

A spotted Tomcat is stretching his body on the floor. His name is Tomcat.

Narrator:

>"Pussy, pussy! Come here lovely puss!"

Tomcat became spoiled but suddenly spring up to prey a mouse that is peeking into the pot.

Narrator:

>"He hasn't been catch mouse the pest so far. (*addressed to the camera*) Let's go to the other case."

Sequence 10:

INT. STABLE - Day

Narrator:

> "Well, here is Farmer's stable."

<S> Out of the stable. The camera pulls in the stable.

A Horse has wrapped a towel around his neck. He is boxing and swimming. He is cleaning his sweat. He is combing his curly mane. Also He is drinking water then combing his forelock to the left of his forehead. But his forelock fell on his forehead, again.

Narrator:

> "The last place where I must show you is a piggy
>
> House belonged to Two Brothers. They owner
>
> a small restaurant in middle of green Pansy."

Sequence 11:

EXT. Piggy house - Day

<S> The uncovered yard of the piggy house where has surrounded by wooden fences. In the yard two pigs and five fat and pink piglets live. Piglets are following each other. They are playing with each other tail and tie them. They do curling them, then forming straight them. They are throwing mud to each other and laughing.

Narrator:

> "Ah... what a round pounded meat! (*addressed*
>
> *to the* piglets) Goochy, Goochy! May God keep you.
>
> They ravished my heart. Oh! Where is Mr. Piggy?
>
> My God! He has sat at the corner alone. Because
>
> he has suffered from depression. Did you say 'why'?
>
> Ok! Wait a few minutes, please!"

Sequence 12:

EXT. PANSY VILLAGE (OPEN- VIEW) - DAY

<L S> Pansy village.

<S> A shot of opening the doors of; cottages, stables, chicken coops, green grocery, restaurant, tailor store and...

Lady Tailor is an elegant set up, well, beautiful and smartly dressed orders the clothes. Now she is scattering seeds for Duck and Ducklings in the yard store. Priest is sprinkling seed for Cock, Hen and her Chicks, too. Greengrocer opened the door of his store and then went on the roof. He opened the door of pigeon coop and now he is releasing them to fly.

Narrator:

"Oh... I had forgotten the Pigeons. Of course they

played an important role in the village adventures."

Farmer closed his Horse to the cart to take to the farm. His wife put his lunch-pack into the cart. Miller took his donkey in to the mill, and the donkey's Foal is playing in meadow around the mill.

Lady Gardener kissed Grocer and then she is going to gardening in her rose garden. Grocer opened his grocery near the garden. Two brothers have leaned on their chairs at their restaurant balcony and are listening to the radio. Their cheeks and noses are red because of drunkenness. Priest dusts the church then he lights a candle.

Little Shepherd is bringing cows, sheep, goat and their children to the field. A sheep-dog by the name of Miss Poop is guarding them severely, too. Zak is paying attention to Lady Tailor, completely. Lady Tailor is buffing the window of her store. Zak is looking at her elegant body lovely. He is so gazing to her that he is going back to look her more than.

Sequence 13:

INT. PANSYPEOPLE'S BEDROOMS - DAY

The Narrator:

"The story began from that day morning. That day

the Cock didn't sing for first time and all people

overslept."

<M S> People of Pansy, who have slept in different positions. These plans are shown as painting and fixed pictures.

--Open mouth--Laying face downwards--Head and body are under bed sheet except feet--Bowing down--One of two eyes is open and other eye is close--Supine. And hands are under head and one of legs is on another leg

<M S> People's surprised faces. These plans are shown as painting and fixed pictures.

--Open mouth--Circular eyes--Raised eyebrows--Biting their fingers--Scratching their heads--Erect hair--Their hands on their waists--With palm toward up

Sequence 14:

EXT. PANSY VILLAGE- DAY

<L S> Pansy village.

Narrator:

"At first people thought they were abducted, but

no long time they understood that..."

<S> Two brothers' radio.

The radio narrator:

"From beginning of this morning domestic animal

from all villages in a pre-programmed plan

gathered together in front of building of ARSA,

animals' rights support association. The

demonstration, they are saying this motto: Stop

animal persecution!"

INT. LADY TAILOR'S TAILORING STORE - DAY

Lady Tailor and some her customers have stood in front of TV.

TV monitor is broadcasting live; Some pictures about a great crowd of people, animals and reporters who are reporting about animals walking and demonstration. Pansy animals have dressed up (formal clothes) and they are in the first line.

A lady reporter is waiting for the record of the program has not started still, tells photographer:

> "Gorge! Take a picture from that cow... it's interesting."

Lens is zoomed on Mrs. Cow with a placard with this motto:

> "Stop to insult."

Lady reporter:

> "No! Not Mrs. Cow, Her husband."

Lens is zoomed on Mr. Bull with a placard with this motto:

> "Stop to oppress us."

Lady reporter:

> "Oh Gorge! I mean the fish."

There is a fishbowl with a Goldfish on Mr. Bull's head. Lens is zoomed on that. Gold fish blows several bubbles as large as a balloon. Bubbles contain some pictures of dead whales and dolphins in bloody sea and this motto:

- "Are all old customs right?"
- "Penguins and Polar bears are sons of pole. Don't make artificial environment in zoo for them."
- "Stop taxidermy".

Continuously Gold fish is wearing oxygen mask on his mouth and standing on the fishbowl's edge and also it`s flying them into the air. Bubbles are so big that Mr. Bull is close to take off. Lens is zoomed on the other placards.

Sheep's placard:

> "Stop to torment animals; Forbidden torment
>
> animals."

Cock's placard:

> "Hey man! Give up selfishness!"

Turkey's placard:

> "We have both personality and feeling."

Sow's placard:

> "We are God creatures, too."

Billy goat's placard:

> "The man and animals God is the same."

A white cat that has worn mask, because of being unknown, is trying to escape from the camera. She hid herself among people. Animals' mottos are mixing with the sounds of their Children; baa, baa, ma, ma, aarr, aarr…

Sequence 16:

EXT. PANSY VILLAGE - DAY

Pansy people are wondered.

Everybody says something.

Talking voice:

-   "What did we insult them?"

-   "What oppression do they tell about it?"

-   "What do they mean?"

-   "I can't understand it. Absolutely they don't

    like their live."

-     "They are so rude. What do animal oppression

  and insulting mean?"

-     "Well, they are animal.

-     "Do animals understand?"

-     "Now, they understand. They understand deeply."

Sequence 17:

EXT. IN FRONT OF ARSA (ANIMALS' RIGHTS SUPPORT ASSOCIATION) BUILDING (CITY) - DAY

The Anti-Riot police have lined up in front of the demonstrators and prevented them to enter to the building. Photographers and reporters from different TV and radio stations are reporting intensively. The Police chief is a middle-aged man and has worn sunglasses.

The Police chief (*by his handy-speaker*):

>"Dear animals! Please don't ruin security in a city.
>
>Come back to your homes, now. Otherwise I am
>
>forced to command to arrest and put you in the
>
>cage."

Horse (*neighs and starts to speak loudly and politely*):

>"We don't want to revolt and ruin security of city.
>
>We just want to speak to Head of our association
>
>to support us. It's not so much expectation. Is it?"

All animals (*talking*):

-     "Yes! We must speak to the head."

-     "It's our rights."

-     "Here is the supporting of Animals' rights Association.

  It means: our rights."

-     "If we can't see the head, we will not come back to

our nests."

The Police chief:

> "My friends! Please don't deceive enemies. Don't
>
> gather together here for instigation your friendly-
>
> faced enemies, and don't risk your life."

Sequence 18:

INT. HEAD'S BEDROOM - DAY

Head has slept in his bed. His telephone is ringing. He is bending to take the phone. The phone was being thrown out of the window that The Head plunged to take it into the air like a goalkeeper. While he has hanged off the edge of the window, he starts to speak by phone.

The voice on the phone:

> "Please come to the association quickly, sir!
>
> Animals revolted. They insist to speak to you,
>
> certainly."

Head (*sleepy*):

> "What do they want?"

The voice:

> "They told nothing, but they wrote some words
>
> About insulting on their placards."

Head (*yawning*):

> "Ok, tell them to write their complaint and give
>
> them to the secretaries. When I come there, I will
>
> read and investigate their complaint."

The voice:

> "But it seems you didn't take notice of it. Ten
>
> thousand groups of domestic animals gathered

together."

Head (*interrupted the voice words on the phone, worried, wondered and shouted*):

"Ten thousand groups?!"

Head (*jumped out of his bed quickly and shouted*):

"Coup! Coup! We must do something very soon."

Sequence 19:

EXT.IN FRONT OF ARSABUILDING (CITY) - DAY

After a minute a black car stopped near the building by strong brake. All of the reporters are running towards the car and surround it. All animals paid attention to it. An old banger car stopped the other side of the building for missing the way.

The handsome and fit Head got off the car quickly, and stood on the stairs of the building. Five Pigeons are flying above the crowd without paying attention.

Head:

"Dear friends! Welcome. I proud that I listen

to you. I am sure that you are right, because I

believe that nice animals such you are right

always. I promise to do everything that I can."

Animals (*moving their placards and shouting*):

"We don't want anything, unless our rights. We

have just a life without insulting and persecution.

We don't want any appreciation."

Head (*to be calm with the finger*):

"It's your birthright."

The crowd is cheering.

Head:

"Just let me…because the hall of association has limited capacity, please send some of your agents indoor for discussion."

A man is murmuring in Head's ear. Head with up eyebrow.

Head (*by speaker*):

"I heard the source of this summit was from Pansy village. So let me invite Pansy people to come to the hall. The others can follow conference too."
(*pointing to a scoreboard that some people are installing on the building*).

The scoreboard is turned on. The hall view is shown.

Head:

"Hey! Pansy's! Please inter the hall. (*looking at the crowd*) In honor of them!"

Everybody is clapping the hands.

The Pansy animals enter toward the hall among the crowd.

Head is going towards the door of hall. Mr. Bull and Mrs. Cow and their Calf are the first animals that are coming towards stairs. Two Pigeons are flying to the hall quickly without paying attention to hide among the ceiling luster.

A Policeman (*preventing Calf from entering*):

"No kids!"

Calf took his father's tail and now he is screaming strongly. Also mucus of his nose is flowing and a big air bubble is made by it. The policeman's picture is clear in the bubble. The child jumps up and bursts the bubble.

Bull:

"Children are the part of our life."

Head heard these sounds, so he looked at the back of his head. He is pointing to the police to allow children to enter.

INT. HALL OF ARSA - DAY

Inside the hall is like a court. Head has sat behind a large table up the hall. Twin sister and brother who their names are Titi and Mimi sit the left and the right side of Head.

All animals and one of the Pigeons sit on the benches in the hall. They have worn nice cloths, polished shoes and beautiful hats.

Head:

> "I am listening to you completely. What can I do?
>
> Please start (*looking at Miss Poop*) Why did you
>
> enter with gun? (*in a jeering tone*) We have no dispute
>
> against you. Don't you know to enter this place
>
> with gun is illegal?

Head is pointing to two guards next to the door. Miss Poop has stood like a soldier. She opened the baton from her waist by herself and gave it to the guarders and then sits again.

Head:

> "I want to hear about you Mr. …a…"

Miss Poop (*standing right just a soldier*):

> "I am Miss Poop, sir!"

Head (*surprised*):

> "Oh… How interesting! I am so curious to know
>
> that did you really have a complaint? But you have
>
> important and valuable position among people."

Miss Poop (*bitter smile*):

> "Hearing these words from you it's so wonderful.

Aren't you aware about news and difficulties in

the world? If it's true, I want you to read newspapers

and to search on Internet, please, here you are."

(Miss Poop gave a CD to the Head).

Head gave the CD to Titi. She put it in to a Lap top and played the pictures on the wall. The film is shown different parts of tormenting dogs in different societies. Mimi and Titi put their hands on their eyes because they don't want to see these pictures. Head nodded, regretfully. Inside and outside the hall, people's eyes are full of tears. Some animals can't stand to see this film. Some of them closed their children's eyes to not see this film. And some are cleaning their tears by tissue.

Head:

"Enough! Please!"

Titi paused playing.

Miss Poop (*shocking*)**:**

"For what sin? Why does man allow to treat God

creatures such behavior by himself /herself?

Who does say that God created us to serve man?

Yes, we have good symbiosis with mans and help

 them so much including; To save their life under

the debris.

To help the blinds and … Is it your appreciation?

How about police dog?

In some societies we are known as unclean

creatures. Are we unclean or some people in

humanity mask who kill thousands of children

and good people of their own kind a tone minute!?

Sir! Imagine, a person isn't vaccinated on time,

as a result, he falls sick. Do you beat him violently because of his illness, even he is a conductor of the most dangerous virus and bacteria? I don't understand" jumped blood". Does it mean? If a man is injured by a bullet, his blood doesn't jump out? Does it come drop by drop? It's laughable that in some where dog is compared with a liar person and is said he tells lie like dog! Have somebody ever seen or heard that a dog barking means coming a thief and then people notice there isn't a thief?! We have heard the liar shepherd, never the liar dog. Men betray to their spouses or their own kind. They lie for reaching to their goals. They lie to make easier their life and to solve daily problems. people who hear lie, and see betrayal, unfaith and unclean in us, actually are seeing their inner states. Hey man! Be honest! Tell the truth! Be faithful! Don't betray! Be a clean heart!"

Animals inside and outside of the hall are clapping the hands.

Miss Poop took up a placard that, with these written words on it;

"The white lie is a kind of mask on the face"

During the show, everything is under a one's eyes surveillance. The one's eyes are mysterious, shiny, nice and two colors. One of the eyes is blue and another is black. One's body and face is hided in the darkness. All animals became free from clapping the hand and now they sit without speaking.

Head (*looking at* ***The audience***):

> "Your words were shocking. It is our duty to investigate
>
> your protest."

Miss Poop is experiencing a feeling of honor and victory at the same time. Her eyes are shining.

The crowd is applauding her. (whistling and clapping the hands)

Head:

> "Well, Excellency the Mr. Bull! I'm ready to hear
>
> your words..."

Suddenly the noises are heard out of the hall.

Head (*looking at Mimi*):

> "What's the matter? Please consider that!"

Mimi put hands free microphone on his ears. The hands free are connected to a Laptop. Mimi is murmuring at the microphone.

Mimi (*looking at Head*):

> "Sir! People of pansy village want to arrive here
>
> forced to take their animals. They are pushing
>
> the door as hard as they can."

<C S> Animals worried face and their talking.

Miss Poop (*looking at animals*):

> "Don't worry my friends! Here is our rights support
>
> association. Here's peaceful. Nobody can hurt us here."

He-ass:

> "If man had understood the law and rights, now we
>
> wouldn't have been here."

EXT. IN FRONT OF ARSA BUILDING - DAY

People of Pansy village are trying to open the door of the saloon to arrive. The Police prevent them to arrive.

<M S> The scoreboard on the wall of the street. The Scoreboard is showing Head. He took the hands free from Mimi and put on his ears.

Head:

"Dear people of nice Pansy village! Please listen to me for a few minutes! (*people of Pansy stopped and are watching the scoreboard*) Your animals are in peace and security. They have sat inside the hall. Don't worry about them. Please be quiet. You are angry and may hurt them. You know that nobody has right to hurt animals. The law always supports animals".

People of Pansy (*shouting*):

"What's the law? We want our animals. We need them. Our life has stopped."

Head:

"Yes, I know these animals belong to you but they have rights. Please have patience. I will return them when they bring up their requests. This is to your advantage."

People of Pansy grumbled but became quiet soon.

INT. HALL OF ARSA - DAY

Head (*looking at **The audience***):

"Stick to the subject! (*looking at **Bull***) Well, please speak Mr. Bull!"

Bull tightened his tie knot and stood up.

Sequence 23:

EXT. INFRONT OF ARSABUILDING - DAY

<S> **Grocer** (*looking at* **Lady Gardener**):

> "Oh, he is our Bull. We didn't expect him to do it."

Suddenly Bull pulled a cleaver from his inside breast pocket quickly. Head, Mimi, Titi and the crowd shocked.

Head, Mimi, Titi, The audience:

> "Oh! My God!"

Calf has nursed. Suddenly Calf turned his head towards The audience. He looked at his father, and then the cleaver went on to nurse.

Bull (*heaved a loud roar like a lion and showed the cleaver*):

> "One (*pulled a red towel from the pocket*) Tow; harm;
>
> three; insult. My wife will explain perfectly."

Head:

> "Mr. Bull! You must not to bring that deadly weapon
>
> here. (*winking*) In front of the children...please..."

<C U> Ducklings, Chicks, Calf, Lamb and Kid.

When Head winked two guards to come towards Bull and took the cleaver. Calf stops to nurse and turns his head towards head.

Calf:

> "You can use to kill us, but my father
>
> must not bring that here. Even for a document
>
> against Man."

Bull:

> "You haven't mercy on our children and part them

from their mothers in tears and..." (*copies to cut*

himself head without any word in front children to not

notice.)

But Calf understood, so shaking and griped his mother.

<S> Chicks have step in a foursome baby carriage.

There are some pacifiers in their mouths. Chubby Chick has crowded two Chicks out because she is double sized.

Two thin Chicks opened one of their tow eyes to deliberate conditions. They are planning to escape. Chubby Chick has slept deeply. Two thin Chicks put their pillows under the blankets. Because they want their mother to think they have slept. Then two thin Chicks went down the baby carriage without speaking. Once they began to walk on the floor, their legs are pulled back. They felt fear because they thought their mother has entrapped them. But at once they understood their legs, has tied to Chubby Chick's leg by a string.

Chubby Chick is waving her hand in to air. She put her pillow under the blanket, too. Then she tied her doll to herself and tried to go down the baby carriage hardly. To go down is difficult for her, because she is fat. Chubby chick's brothers are helping her to go the baby carriage. Three Chicks are getting away from there. The Cow is raising her hand with diffidence.

Head (*allowed **her** to speak*):

"Dear lady! I'm interested to hear your words."

Cow:

"Sir! My husband and I want to say about

slaughtering and butchery and sheep's head

and trotters and cleaver and knife..."

Head (*surprised*):

"Go on please...!"

Cow:

"These problems aren't very disputable. Maybe
God's primary goal in creating us is this. But
we can't accept insult or harm."

Head:

"Your dear family told that."

Cow:

"No Sir! They didn't tell all problems in some countries,
people worship us. But in some lands of the world,
people wound us for hobby and happiness. When
they want to curse at someone use our name. Also
when they like to charge someone with folly and say;
you are folly like Cow. I have a question! Which one
of our acts is the sign of folly? Whereas in this same
city, one time, we went to metro. Oh! My god! We saw
so many things."

Sequence 24:

(FLASH BACK)

INT. METRO STATION - DAY

A train stopped. Some passengers are going to get on and off the train
forcedly.

The passengers are protesting in the wagons:

"You have to allow us to get off, then you get on."

But the protests did not work. The doors are closed and the train moved,
finally. All passengers are angry and curse.

Flashback: <The images have adjusted to the Cow's narration>

Cow:

"It was made us laugh. I told my husband; really

these people don't know that if passengers get

wagons off in turn and allow to others to come in,

as a result they can get on easily." (*a bitter laughter*)

But say us folly."

Calf:

"But we aren't folly. Because when we hear the

sounds of emergency vehicles sirens, we get

out of their way. (*standing and protesting*) Really!

Some drivers say to the driver next to them:

"Hey calf! Why do you tell them calf? That driver isn't a

child. Is that? A proverb was known; whom I don't

know was born like a calf and died like a Cow.

Please investigate that, sir!"

All animals are applauding Calf.

Sequence 25:

EXT. INFRONT OF ARSA BUILDING - DAY

Lady Gardener (*clapping the hands and laughing*):

"You are a one! What a chick!"

Grocer (*interrupted her words*):

"Shush, shush! Don't say the chick! If they hear it, they

will protest about this word."

Lady Gardener (heedless of **Grocer**):

"Well down!"

Grocer (*looking at **Lady Gardener***):

"His sarcasm was aimed at you."

Lady Gardener (*surprised*):

> "At me?"

Grocer:

> "Yes, you always say that drivers don't allow you to
>
> pass the calf."

Lady Gardener looked at her husband, angrily.

Sequence 26:

INT. HALL OF ARSA - DAY

Head:

> "Sorry! I will certainly investigate that."

Mimi is writing some things on a paper quickly. Titi is typing them on her Laptop quickly.

Sequence 27:

EXT. INFRONT OF ARSA BUILDING - DAY

The scoreboard is showing the Pigeon:

> "Man has taken away our liberty from us and has
>
> changed into captivity. Because man thinks that
>
> who is the owner of the world. Man wants to take
>
> control everything, even our rate of flight. So Man
>
> clips our wings.
>
> Whereas creatures have no right to negate beings
>
> liberty. The liberty is a divine blessing. The negation
>
> of the liberates of beings is to offend against rules of
>
> nature."

All of animals and some people of Pansy are applauding and pulling for the Pigeon.

Greengrocer (*angrily*):

> "I wish I would cut your tongue, too."

The scoreboard is showing Hen, Cock and the baby carriage. Hen and Cock have stood up and they are ready to speak. Priest smiled when he saw them. Then he closed his eyes and crossed his hands for them.

People of Pansy village (*surprised*):

–   "Do they have a complaint against priest?

     I can't believe that priest has harmed them."

–   "He is a man of god."

–   "When a priest harms animals, what do you expect

     from other people?"

–   "Be quiet! Allow to hear what they say."

People became quiet. Cock has stood up. His legs are shaking.

Cock (*looking at the head in a vibrating voice, starting to speak*):

     "Thanks for your permission! If you want the truth,

     I can't speak, too. Because of seeing The audience,

     I have been afraid. Then I ask my dear wife to bring up

     the family complaint."

Sequence 28:

INT.HALL OF ARSA BUILDING - DAY

Hen smiled satisfactorily. She is very pleased. She is arranging her scarf and ready to speak. Once she opened her mouth suddenly, Cock is starting to Speak.

Cock:

     "Following dear Calf words, I repine at many eggheads.

     Superstitious people kill us. They are rich and buy

     expensive cars. But they believe blood of black cock

     brings good luck. A black cock is an offering for their

own new cars. They say this blood protects their cars against accident."

Head is surprised and his lip hung.

Hen (*murmuring on the **Cock's** ear*):

"It is enough! Leave it to me! You have stress, so you can't complain entirely."

Cock:

"Thank you my kind wife! Please ..."

Hen (*seeking to play it, cool*)**:**

"No! Please! Boil it down."

Cock (*afraid of **Hen**, forced to smile*):

"Your wish is my command! A proverb was known: ladies first."

Cock face got red because of shame.

Hen (*smiling and arranging **her** scarf again*):

"Thank you darling! (*looking at Head*) Head! I want to thank Priest because he looks after us well. We have no grievance against him. But (**Hen** *personality changed perfectly. **She** is giving a speech bravely like Hitler. So Hitler's face appeared in **The audience's** mind*) I have a grievance. I representing my family and the in the world, organic and machinery chickens, I say that we aren't afraid of to be roasted (*doing over reaction and cleaning **her** tears*) as Mr. Bull say that may be is our destiny (*in a brisk voice*) but we hate to be hurt. Man offense us.

They call talkative ladies: hen! Is a hen a talkative bird?

Does a hen have a bad sound? No I don't think so.

It is a gift. I cluck after laying an egg and also call

my family by this voice. Doesn't God bestow every

one a sound to acclaim others? "

Cock (*looked at **Hen** surprisingly. Then **he** is murmuring on **her** ear*):

"That's enough! Feel the room! Don't carry away!"

< E C U > A pair of nice, shiny and mysterious eyes, in to darkness at the corner of the wall. One of eyes is black and that one is blue.

Hen (*looking at **Cock***):

"I`m not finished, still, sir! (*looking at **Head***)

Some people are so rude and even use our names

for their meaningless proverb."

Chubby Chick is walking to put her doll to sleep, at last. Her brothers have to follow her. Every time Chubby Chick is returning her brothers fall down on the floor because their legs are pulled back. Hen affective tune has impressed Head and he is trying to speak in literary like Hen.

Head:

"What proverbs? ... Give an example?"

The audience and Hen are looking at Head surprisingly.

Hen:

"Oh! My God! So rough! I didn't expect this from you.

Stick to the subject. For example; hen has one leg.

(***She** is raising **her** leg and showing it to **Head***) Do I really

have one leg?"

Head, Mimi and Titi are imaging her as Fried chicken for a minute, then they licked their mouths.

Mimi (*murmuring*):

> "Wow!..."

Titi (*murmuring*):

> "Mmm…"

Head (*murmuring*):

> "Yaaammm"

Lamb:

> "Evert your eyes!"

Hen is bringing down her leg. She is bringing out her Chicks of the baby carriage to show their legs.

Hen:

> "Do my Chicks really have one leg?"

Suddenly Hen understood pillows were in her brass instead of her Chicks. Hen looked at the Cock, angrily. Cock is going like the clappers, finding their Chicks. The Chicks are staring at a pair of shy eyes, one black and that one blue, into darkness. Cock is staring at the eyes, too. Suddenly Cock pecks at the eyes. The owner of the eyes screamed and ran away. The scream sound caused to silence in the saloon.

Head:

> "Is there any problem Your Excellency, the Cock?"

Cock:

> "No sir! A…A… Yes, sir! There is another problem.
>
> Man accuses us cocks for two crimes: 1: polygamy.
>
> That's to say; every cock has many wives.
>
> 2: Man even accuses us to share our wives among
>
> other cocks; you see!... It`s so awful.
>
> That's to say; The cocks have joint ownership
>
> about hens. But these events are happened in

human society. I sure you have heard about the men who that have many wives. That's to say; One man has several wives. (*paused*) Some husbands give over their wives to other men for money. (*putting Chicks into the baby carriage*) And find point! A question! Why do some idlers waste their time in order to watch a cock fighting race?"

Hen (*beating up on **herself***):

"Tell some Man who believe their neighbor's hen is goose. They are delusional. I think they are addicted to marijuana."

Head (*surprised*):

"What?"

Cock:

"That means the apples on the other side of the wall are sweeter than the others."

Hen (*is crying and brings out **her Chicks** of baby carriage again*):

"Is that fair? My Chicks… (*understood those are pillows. **She** threw them towards **Cock**. **Cock** took them in his arms*) Man cooks chicken soup… Oh no! My God! My poor Chicks! No… no…" (*weeping and passing out*)

At once Cock plucks some his feathers and spreads them on the bench. Then he helped Hen to sit on feathers. He plucked a feather of Hen tail and blew her by feather.

Hen (*feeling comfort*):

"Clucking…"

Suddenly Hen understood that Cock has plucked her tail. She took the feather angrily. Hen is laying a big egg because of this action. Cock took the egg proudly and now he is showing it to Head.

Cock:

> "Her clucking arises out of this egg. (*looking at* **Hen**)
>
> Let me give it to you. (*is giving the egg to* **Head**) Your
>
> respectfully."

Head (*looking at big egg surprisingly*)**:**

> "Wow! What a big egg!"

Hen (*feeling ashamed tinged with proud*)**:**

> "It is especially for you, sir."

Mimi and Titi are licking their mouths.

Head:

> "Ok! Stick to the subject."

Sequence 29:

EXT. INFRONT OF ARSA BUILDING (AT THE CORNER) - DAY

Blue eye of Female cat has got red with blow of Cock peck. She crept out of the hole at the corner <hidden hole> and is scratching her eye.

She is hearing the noises, looking at there. A spotted Tomcat is disputing with a police officer.

Female cat (*murmuring by* **herself**)**:**

> "What a beautiful cat! You are the man of my dreams."

Police officer (*looking at* **the Tomcat**)**:**

> "Sorry! just the animals of Pansy village."

Tomcat:

> "I'm from Pansy village, too."

Police officer (*doubtfully*)**:**

"Where have you been so far?"

Tomcat:

"As always in chase criminal mice."

Police officer:

"Sorry, it's too late. You have no permission to

enter the saloon because your entrance can

cause confusion."

Tomcat:

"That's unfair (*looking at the scoreboard*) because

There is no cat inside. Who will defend cat rights?"

Police officer:

"Sorry! As I told before, your entrance to the

Saloon is forbidden. Leave here please.

Follow the meeting on scoreboard."

At all this time Female cat is looking at Tomcat deeply. She is whistling slowly.

Tomcat hears her whistle an, looking at her. She winked at him means to follow her.

Tomcat is going towards her.

Female cat (*showing the hole*)**:**

"This way please."

Tomcat (*looking at the scoreboard*)**:**

"Why didn't I see you there?"

Female cat:

"Because I have no complaint against Man. My

owner takes care of me very well."

Tomcat:

"It is selfishness. You must think all cats in the

world, and their problems. Not just yourself.

All cats aren't lucky like your mademoiselle.

Have you ever heard about to castrate cats?"

Female cat is staring at him surprisingly.

Tomcat *(desperately)*:

"Oh! Sorry! What a strange word! Some people

have not mercy on themselves. They circumcise

even their little daughters and believe women

only have to give birth, without enjoyment sex.

(before creeping into the hole, stopped a moment,

*and looked at **her**)* Thank you."

He is going to the hall. She is following him.

Sequence 30:

INT. HALL OF ARSA BUILDING - DAY

Tomcat is sneaking under benches soundless and quickly. Nobody saw him. He sat down next to He- ass. Female cat hided at darkness again. Suddenly Ram and Billy goat hold their children's arms. Ram and Billy-goat, Lambs, and Kid stood up.

Billy-goat *(showing the **Kid** to **Head**)*:

"sir! Look at this! Please look at him! Please

Head! Please look at this Kid's eyes! His innocent

eyes! He has a pure and lovely look. Doesn't he?"

<E C U> Kid`s unruly eyes. Kid stared at Head's eyes. An impolitely and shamelessly look. Then Kid plucked only long tail of Hen hurtfully and slyness, and put it on his head like Indian.

Billy-goat (*continues*):

"How can you eat this attractive child?"

Ram (*chocking with tears and looking at **Lamb***):

"How can you roast this innocent child?"

<C U>

Lamb is keeping pock his noise. Head is looking at Lamb reluctantly. Lamb is rounding his noise wax and then shooting the bullet into the air. Head is looking for the bullet wax. It is rolling into the air and coming down Mimi's mouth. Because Mimi is yawning, When the bullet was coming down in his mouth he closed his mouth. Mimi felt a thing into his mouth then chewed and tasted that. He pulled out a piece of bullet wax and looked at that. Then he put that in his mouth again and chewed it during meeting.

Ram:

"Cooking (*showing **Billy-goat***) my cousin and

changing into (*pushed **his** hair and showed **his***

teeth like slaughtered) Sheep's head and trotters

or broth is acceptable. But our children…

(*copied to cut his head* without speaking but

Billy-goat did not understand*) no… at all…"

Billy-goat:

"Last month my niece telephoned me. She

told me just as was weeping; At a cursed

festival and superstition custom…

(*chocking with tears*) Men carried her father

on their hands and pulled His arms and legs

in four directions… (*bursting into tears, sitting*

down on the bench and murmuring) Oh my poor

brother!"

Ram (*is massaging **Billy-goat**'s shoulders*):

> "Just for happiness and good fortune."

Billy-goat is weeping loudly. The audience is bringing down their heads without speaking sadly. Turkey face is parti-colored because she is weeping hardly.

Head (*looking at Turkey*):

> "It's your turn now, lady!"

Titi (*in jeering tone murmuring **herself***):

> "Lady rainbow!"

Titi is laughing in her sleeve. As she is laughing in a low tone and her tears are running down her eyes. Then her face is getting like a rainbow. Suddenly Titi stopped because of showing her face on the Laptop. She cleaned her face at once but it became like a babyish painting. She felt poverty and despondency.

Turkey (*standing up and saying flirty*):

> "To change colors! It means changeable. It means
>
> chameleonic. Whereas they themselves are
>
> hypocritical liar, and spy for enemy. Man has
>
> masked. Their behavior and words are
>
> diametrically opposed in the house and out
>
> the house. They don't comb their hair but when
>
> want to get out of house to spruce up themselves.
>
> It means they trim up.
>
> It means they change from devil into fairy. I'm happy
>
> because I'm not a man of too many faces. My colors
>
> are sign of greatness of God. How about you, Man?"

Turkey took up a placard that, with these written on:

> "No hard luck story. Just be yourself!"

<C U> The meek and sad face of Sow. The Pig has stared at a distant and unknown point without speaking.

Sow (*submissively*)**:**

> "Is it a boar? In many countries name me; boar. Because the people don't like to mention my name. They believe I am unclean. Even when announcers of those countries dub animations without mentioning my name. But such people from that land have prospected their children to have promising future, with such mistake knowledge."

The Crowd is laughing loudly. Mimi and Titi are sneering.

He-ass:

> "Oh, my God! This is very, very, very…ver…ry… fu … nnn…nyyy…! The… funniest … joke… in the… world! (*is laughing hardly*) ha! Ha…they …name …ha, ha, ha…soo …ow…b…b…bo… boarrr…ha, ha…"

Foal (*laughing*)**:**

> "I laughed my guts out."

Sow (*loudly*)**:**

> "They call me lazy. Whereas themselves want to become rich in one night. Because they like to lean on sofa and to watch TV at night and day (*in jeering tone*) to live in lazily, lasting their life.(*shouting*) Hey Man!

Your wife dispatches you to take a bath.
There are some men that after bathing, wear
same previous sweaty clothes again. You
don't wash your fetid sock. Your fetid sweat
body bothers other passengers in metro.
Hey woman! You are a fop, nice perfumed at
outside house. Are you at home, too? Do you
clean and all made up? And arranged hair?
(*shouting hardly*) Man! Take a shower!"

The audience is applauding her (whistling and clapping the hands). Then
they are laughing, too.

A voice between The audience:

"Keep us laughing on a boot."

Another voice between The audience:

"I laughed my guts out."

Sow (*loudly*):

"My husband is suffering from depression
because of standing these all pain."

The audience became quite even Head.

Duck (*put headphones on **Ducklings** ears*):

"I don't like my Ducklings to hear my words
because these words don't befit them. (*looking
at **Head***) Sir! We always move in a line and
man mock our order and regularity instead
of they to learn us this good act and do that
at the time to get on and off bus or taxi.

They have a proverb; to trick by duck.

That means to look woman as a commodity.

They misuse duck in order to trick, to attract

at last and to hunt other drakes."

Ducklings (*at once*)**:**

"What a hateful act! What a shameful conduct!"

Duck (*surprised*)**:**

"Have you heard my words?"

Ducklings (*at once*)**:**

"Yes mom!"

Duck:

"How?"

Ducklings (*at once*)**:**

"You forgot to play music for us."

Horse stood up.

Head (*unreal surprising*)**:**

"Mr. Horse? Have you any complaint, too?

Against whom? Man calls you gentle."

Horse:

"I prefer they don't hoot us. Man is careless

and kills a lot of creatures (people, animals

and birds) by his madly driving. They

themselves name horsy act this kind of

driving. Whereas if our children to run like

their driving we remind them; Run like a horse,

not like Man! You know? Man is a thankless

creature. While a creature is serviceable for
them. They made work at the end of life.
But once they understand that creatures can't
work keep away them. Even in order to grow
old or illness. It doesn't make any difference.
Whether a horse or their parents."

The audience is sad. Head is thinking. Mimi and Titi are yawning.

He-ass (*standing up and clapping the hands*):

"You can say that again. Please give a warm
Welcome to Mr. Horse."

The audience has stood up and they are clapping the hands.

He-ass:

"We work our tail off like horses. We are
Good Porters and good mount. Even
feces of a pregnant female donkey is an
effective antibiotic. To arrive the stable,
we line up. We neither push out each
other nor tread. We never fight one
another for an extra basket of straw. We
don't like to go to veterinary clinic for it."

Foal (*quickly*):

"Daddy! Daddy! Please tell me; when Men
want to cuss their children say foal. Why?"

The audience (*laughing and adoring **Foal** and giving it kiss*):

"You are as well as gold. We will be glad
like you."

Foal cheeks got red. His black eyes are shining. His thick eyelashes became wet. Lamb raised his hand.

Head (*kindly with* **Lamb**)**:**

>"Taste…ha…a… tell, please, tell."

Lamb:

>"No rodeo. No bullfighting. Oh, my mind is kindling
>
>at the thought of these audacities."

The audience is applauding him.

Tomcat (*standing up*)**:**

>"My mother was a house cat in this city. No a
>
>vagrant cat. When she conceived, her owners
>
>migrated from that city. They couldn't take her
>
>with themselves. So they abandoned her easily.
>
>My mom couldn't find food in dust bins or to
>
>catch mice. She had no power to fight vagrant
>
>cats for food. Vagrant cats ripped my mom
>
>and I was born. But she died immediately. A
>
>lady found me and took to her home in Pansy
>
>village.
>
>She took care of me. Yes, Men are selfish. When
>
>they need us animals, take care of us. Otherwise
>
>they abandon simply. That means for animals
>
>deprived of natural life."

Flashback: <The images have adjusted to the Tomcat's narration>

Female cat (*cleaning* **her** *tears and murmuring*)**:**

>"Sorry darling! I promise to be a nice Couple for

you. My love will cause you to forget your past bitter events."

Tomcat (*sneering*)**:**

"This is funny that Man has a proverb' Robber cat'. Whereas man steals indifferent forms, highway robber, pilferer, pirate, purloiner for black mailing, kidnapper, hijacker, burglar, plagiarist, pickpocket, crook and etc.
Men freely embezzle and their embezzlements become to be the daily news headline of the world."

Head (*murmuring*)**:**

"Shut up! Damn!"

Goldfish bubbles:

"Separate the trashes from each other."
"Stop eating live animals. This is painful"

Head (*looking at* **Goldfish** *and* **his** bubbles with a loud voice)**:**

"You Informed us with your silent protests either. (*playing prank on* **animals**) I give youth is good news that your message will be heard by people in the world wide. As soon as I will investigate your protest and requests. Don't worry about them, please go back to Pansy and wait for good news. (*looked at* **Mimi** *and* **Titi**) And you! Please return these nobles to Pansy respectfully and kindly.

Do you hear?"

Mimi is waking confused.

Mimi and Titi (*at once*):

"Respectfully and kindly."

Mimi (*yawning*):

"Respectfully and kindly. Oh, I love these words."

Chubby chick:

"Man has no right to call timid persons; chicken,

sheepish, pigeon, goosey"

Head (***Head***'s *eyes are shining*):

"Well down!"

Animals (Inside and outside the hall) are shaking hands, embracing and kissing each other. The complainant Pigeon is flying towards two Pigeons that have hidden in middle of the ceiling luster to consult with them. Then the complainant Pigeon went out of the saloon. But two Pigeons stay same over there again.

Sequence 31:

EXT. INFRONT OF ARSA BUILDING - DAY

Reporters are interviewing people of Pansy.

People of Pansy:

"We are very surprised."

The Police is protecting animals of Pansy that are getting on a scrap lorry.

The Police:

"Gang way! Get out of the way!"

Other animals are throwing flowers towards animals of Pansy and congratulating them their victory. Animals of Pansy are waving their hands in to the air.

Female cat and Tomcat with hands around each other neck, getting on the scrap lorry. The complainant Pigeon went towards two Pigeons that are flying above people. Three Pigeons are consulting with each other. Then the Pigeons are flying towards the scrap lorry as Mimi and Titi can't see them, anymore.

People of Pansy (*protesting*):

"Where are you taking our animals? Return us them."

<M S> **Head** (*Head*'s picture on scoreboard):

"Don't worry about your animals. We are returning

them to Pansy village. But now I ask you come

along the saloon. I'd like to speak with you about

today events. Please! Thank you."

A number of guards is leading people to Pansy saloon. Mimi took the wheel.

Titi (*jumped in the scrap lorry*):

"Fire up! I'm hungry as a wolf."

Mimi is driving at top. Animals are holding a celebration at the back of the lorry. They are singing loudly and dancing happily. Kid jumped on the roof of the driver's cabin of the lorry. He is watching these views. Kid is hearing Titi and Mimi's voices. Pigeons looked at Kid and they are laughing at him.

Sequence 32:

EXT. ROAD - DAY

Mimi (*laughing*):

"It made me laugh when the Head told; respectfully

and kindly (*bringing out a sharp and shiny dagger*)

a few days mmm... mess kebab celebration."

Kid is afraid of the dagger because to see that dagger reminded him Bull cleaver inside the hall. Titi took the dagger angrily and hided that again.

Titi:

"Are you crazy? They may see that."

Mimi and Titi looked at animals in the mirror of lorry.

Mimi:

"Don't worry. They are very busy."

Titi (*angrily*):

"Not breathe a word! Punch it!"

Mimi:

"Ok! (*looking at **animals** in the mirror*) Laugh now!
Laugh! First comes, first saved. We will laugh soon,
too."

Titi (*sneering*):

"Do you rebel against Man? I'll show you. (*looking at
animals in the mirror*) What are they talking about?"

Mimi:

"What difference does it make? They will be eaten
sooner than they think."

Kid heard that. Kid has lain and he is waiting silently to understand their
talking.

Animals are speaking.

Miss Poop (*looking at Tomcat*):

"Hearing your memory called a memory in my
child hood to my mind. I was weaned recently.
Our owner separated me from my mother and
sold me a person. We were tormented for being
away from each other. What bad days we had!
I got used to my new owner, finally. But after two

years one day my old owner came stealthy and stole me, because my mother was affected with depression. Also my new owner didn't agree to sell me. On the part I wanted to stay with my mom and on the other part I missed my new owner. I was confused. And I suffered at that time."

Tomcat:

"I'm sorry!"

Female cat:

"What a bummer!"

Turkey Hen:

"I know a land that in its literary there is a pronoun called 'Tuo' for one person. Also there is other pronoun called 'Shoma' for more than one person. But when people of that land speak with a Stranger say 'Shoma'. Even if the stranger be one person. But if one person be their friend or a member of family, they say 'tuo'. Because they believe using 'tuo' is insult. Isn't that hypocritically?"

Duck (*surprised*):

"such the people call 'tuo' their parents, sister, brother, aunt, uncle and etc."

Lamb:

"Oh! My God! They insult their family."

Piggy:

"Yes!"

Other Piggy:

> "Insulting is impoliteness."

Horse:

> "They say that using 'tuo' for their friends and family is the sign of sincerity. But about strangers is impoliteness."

Foal:

> "Then…ah…insult is same sincerity."

Ram:

> "No children. It's a mistake."

Children are confused and they are looking at each other.

Billy-goat:

> "We must be explained the details about to kill cattle in their ceremonies. For example; mourning or marriage."

Ram:

> "They offer votive for their dead too."

Ducklings *(at once)*:

> "What does mean votive?"

Piggy:

> "It is a strange indeed! Why don't you know that's mean? It means the quick…ah… the living *(looking at Ducklings)* do you understand?"

Ducklings *(at once)*:

> "Yeah! Point taken."

Piggy:

"Ah...ha...ok! The living is cooking food and sending

other world."

Foal (*surprised*)**:**

"Do the dead eat food?"

He- ass:

"Yes! They marry, too. Man says so."

Two thin chick (*at once*)**:**

"Marriage?"

Chubby Chick:

"Whom the dead get married to?"

Piggy (*making a wry and horrible face for scaring children and changing his voice in rush voice*)

"Ghosts."

Cock (*funny*)**:**

"Hey poop! You had better visit a dentist for

a check-up in advance."

Hen:

"That food belongs to man. Not us."

Female cat:

"What's your destiny post-mortem?"

Cow:

"We go out from the man's gut. I don't know about

you because you are non-eating."

Children (*shudder*)**:**

"Oh no... My God! No..."

Tomcat:

"Are we non-eating? Unfortunately, some people

eat us."

Miss Poop:

"In economy cries condition non-eating becomes

eatable."

Female cat:

"Ok! So… difference between wear eatable or no,

depends on the economic situation."

Tomcat (*murmuring*)**:**

"Economic effect."

Sow:

"Always the first thing begins with economy."

Hen:

"I don't know. Perhaps when the living to eat

that food."

Children are looking at each other surprised. Grown-ups are confused and beginning to think.

He- ass:

"It's difficult to digest. No I can't digest that, indeed."

Sow:

"What have you eaten?"

He-ass:

"This is an idiom. I mean to say that I can't understand

how the dead eat food! It is very strange. Isn't it?"

Animals (*thinking surprisingly*)**:**

"Yeah. It is. It is strange, indeed."

INT. HALL OF ARSA BUILDING - DAY

People of Pansy village have sat on the benches and chatters.

Head:

> "Dear friends! I sure when the chips are down.
> Mind your eye! Be aware! This wasn't only a
> simple protest. Mark my words! I know you like
> your animals but they will give you a hard time.
> It's a long story. I beg you to accept my request.
> Forget your animals. It's a big alarm.
> It won't be easy but there is no way out. You have
> to buy other animals."

People of Pansy are protesting (*protester talking*):

- "We like our animals."

- "We have no money to buy other animals. You have
  to pay for them."

- "My mill will be stopped by the time while I buy one
  other He ass."

- "I have five kilograms milk every day. I don't like to
  leave her."

When Head winked at the guards, they offered people a lot of drink.

Head:

> "Don't worry about these matters. I Promise to help
> you. Are you in agreement with interest - free loan?"

People (*at once*):

"Money loaned without interest?"

Head:

"Yes, of course."

Most people are whistling and clapping the hands happily. But some people have protested yet.

Protesters are shouting:

– "Why?"

– "For what reason?"

– "There is no reason why."

– "Why we must forget our animals and buy another animals?"

Head:

"One simple question; Why? But an important answer; Rise of animals' vigilance. Vigilance animals never will obey you blindly. After that they will complain, regularly. Because they have found out the method to reach their wishes.(*Shouting*)They don't answer your purpose. It is necessary to kill them."

People of Pansy are cheering and drinking up.

Head (*shouting*)**:**

"My treat! Let's go out to dinner on my own account! I will give you a kebab and drink as a treat."

People are cheering happily.

Head (*shouting*)**:**

"Onward! Go to the forest! Hurry up!"

People are running out of the saloon wildly. They are singing loudly a song about dinner party. They are getting on their cars just as they are singing.

They are driving like the clappers. Two Pigeons that were hidden inthe middle of the ceiling luster went out. They want to inform animals about this event.

EXT.ROAD - DAY

Titi (*looking at **Mimi***):

> "Mimi! We are approaching the crossroad of woods
>
> and Pansy village. Make ready that damned juice
>
> quickly."

Mimi is mixing kinds of fluid into a jug.

Kid licks his mouth. Mimi dissolved a lot of pills in fluid and plugged his hand to elbow in fluid to mix that. Kid is shuddering to see that.

Mimi (*laughing*):

> "If they drink this juice, they will sleep. Then we will
>
> take them to woods and roast."

Titi (*laughing*):

> "We provide everything so that Head and people of
>
> Pansy join us."

Mimi:

> "This juice will flavor their meat."

Titi (*happily*):

> "They are supposed to be delicious. Baste them
>
> please!"

Billy-goat is dancing. Kid is flings himself to his father's arms. Billy-goat lost his balance and fell down on the floor of the lorry.

Billy-goat (*angrily*):

> "What's the matter? What are you doing? Please be

quite my son! You are a noisy kid. Leave off your

pranks."

Kid's tongue faltered and jabbered strange words.

Kid:

"Li...liq... (*with closed eyes he is pretending to sleep*

*and to snor*e) Liq..."

Animals are busy without paying attention Kid. Billy-goat is keeping on dance.

Bull (*looking at **Billy-goat***):

"Why are you Jump down on his throat? (*hugging **Kid***)

Goochy, goochy, goo! Do you feel sleep darling?

Don't worry! I put you to sleep."

Bull is laying the Kid on his leg.

Kid:

"N...n...no...Lull..."

Bull:

"Lullaby? Ok darling. I see. Ok, I`m going to sing

a lullaby for you. Shut your eyes! (*singing*)

Lullaby...lull... lu..."

Kid (*looking at **Bull** ears*):

"Hey...!"

Bull:

"What's the matter again? (*with a low voice*) Pee-Pee?

Piss?"

Bull is hugging Kid but Kid is hold his ears at once and describing all events for him quickly.

Bull (*going blank*):

"No! Pull the other one!"

Kid:

"Yes!"

Bull:

"Go sleep! You feel sleepy. You are talking
nonsense."

Kid (*insisting in this manner*)**:**

"Yes, yes you heard me."

Bull:

"You don't say."

Kid:

"Yes!"

Bull Shouted in a loud voice like a lion roaring as Mimi braked strongly. Kid
is shaking and jumped on the roof of driver's cabin of the lorry.

Animals lost their balance and Fell down. They matched each other.
Children are screaming. All of Chicks and Duckling are thrown in to the air.
Horse and He-ass are jumping to right and left till to take them in the air
one by one like a goalkeeper.

Animals (*frightened*)**:**

"What's happened?"

Bull (*pulling out **himself** among **other animals**. **He** has held fishbowl on
his head firmly*)**:**

"Don't be alarmed! Nothing! Don't worry!"

Mr. Piggy (*shouted suddenly*)**:**

"Gold fish! Gold fish!"

Gold fish is jumping up and down on the floor of lorry. Mr. Piggy took Gold
fish and put into the fish bowl quickly. Gold fish is swimming.

Sow (*screaming and shouting happily*)**:**

"He began to talk. He be..." (she is passing out)

Kid slides in driver's cabin of the lorry. Mimi and Titi didn't see him because both got off the lorry just as Kid fell in the driver's cabin. Mimi and Titi are going to back of the lorry. Three Pigeons are worried so to come in the driver's cabin to ask about Kid health. Mimi and Titi didn't see the Pigeons, too.

Suddenly Mimi's foot got caught to a stone and the jug of juice is thrown in to the air. But Titi took advantage that.

Titi (*angrily*):

"Slow coach! Shiftless!"

In this short time Pigeons are coming near animals and informing them about people's call quickly. Then they are flying immediately. Animals are shaking. During this time there is no trace of cats.

Bull:

"Be strong! Be brave!"

Kid is climbing the seat of the lorry and going on the roof to peek around. Mimi and Titi have stood behind the lorry now.

Titi (*an unreal laugh*):

"Hey guys! Do you make a party alone? Well, we

make glorious it with a sweet drink."

Mimi (*happily*):

"You're welcome to it!"

At first Titi offered Bull the juice.

Bull (*worried*):

"If I tell you truth, I'm on diabetic."

All animals are shaking. The Billy-goat has hidden at the corner and is shaking.

Horse:

"I'm feeling puny."

Sow:

"I'm on diet because I have put onseven grams."

Cock (*frightened and panicky*)**:**

"I'm on the pill."

Hen (*interrupted* **Cock** *word*)**:**

"No darling! I'm on the pill... you..."

Cock (*interrupted* **Hen** *word*)**:**

"Oh! Sorry! The juice is hurtful for my vocal cord."

Duck:

"I had a heart attack last year."

Foal:

"I, I...s... (*Has forgotten the word*)s..."

He- ass (*whispering*)**:**

"Sprain."

Foal (*interrupted his father's word loudly and got cold free*)**:**

"Straighten."

Animals, Titi and Mimi are looking at the Foal surprisingly.

He-ass (*loudly*)**:**

"He sprained his ears."

Ducklings (*at once*)**:**

"Our blood pressure is too high."

Chicks:

"Our blood pressured is too low."

Lamb:

"I have gotten diarrhea or I'm constipated. I'm

not sure."

Turkey Hen has passed out in a supine position and her feet are up.

Titi (*screaming*)**:**

"Diabetic, diet, strai...to sprain, diarrhea and...

(*thinking*)... and..."

Mimi (*quickly*)**:**

"Constipation."

Titi:

"Yes. And to pass out are forbidden. Even to think.

You all have to drink this juice."

Mimi (*murmuring*)**:**

"Yes. You have to drink because this juice flavors

you. Don't be shy. Here you are."

Titi (*shouting in a brisk voice*)**:**

"Now!"

Animals are shaking.

Ram (*took the jug quickly*)**:**

"Take it as it comes."

Billy-goat (*Shouting with a loud voice like the roar of a lion*)**:**

"Nooo... (*passing out*).

Suddenly animals shouted and rushed forward Mimi and Titi. They are bucking, clawing, biting, kicking and pecking. Several times it is closed fishbowl to fall down Mr. Bull's head. Pigeons are pecking Mimi and Titi's eyes. Mimi and Titi are running away in the driver's cabin hardly. Animals are chasing them. When, Mimi and Titi took the dagger and a knife. Animals are shaking.

Hen (*shouting like Hitler*)**:**

"Be brave! Attack! Go for it! Seeing Hen called

Hitler In animals mind again. So they rush forward

Mimi and Titi again."

Animals talking:

- "Go for it!"

- "Artful persons!"

- "It was a relief!"

- "Once number is up."

- "I make minces eat out of you."

- "It serves you right!"

Titi:

"Oh, no, no, no..."

Mimi:

"When the chips are down."

All of them are bloody. Some of them are wounded. During this time two Pigeons that were hidden in the middle of the ceiling luster are approaching and informing three Pigeons to go to people.

Pigeons are looking at the end of the road. Some cars carrying people of Pansy village are coming. Police and Head are coming, too. They are shaking shiny knifes and barbecue skewers in to the air. They are singing aloud the same song about party. Four Pigeons are seeking to make barriers on enemy's preceding.

A Pigeon is flying to woods quickly to ask wild beasts to help. Most of the animals are fighting. When Mr. Bull attacked Mimi, he was dodging. So Mr. Bull fell down on the ground. Also fishbowl is thrown on the floor and breaks, too. Goldfish is jumping up and down among the green grass because he can't breathe easily. Ms. Duck became confused.

Children:

"Please put Goldfish under the care of us. We take

him with ourselves."

Mr. Duck put Goldfish into Foal packsaddle and directs children to run away towards woods. She is keeping on fighting. Children disappeared among the grassland. During children are running Goldfish blows bubbles and flies them in to the air hardly. But minute by minute size of the bubbles is becoming small and smaller.

Sequence 35:

EXT.WOODS - DAY

Suddenly a fox is making the mouth water, seeing children.

Fox:

> "mmm… what a delicious food! It's a real turn up
>
> for the books."

Children are falling down because they are very tired. Goldfish is thrown on the floor and jumped up and down again. He is breathing his last so blows a few small bubbles difficulty:

–   "Combat against ignorance!"

–   "Don't forget rights of animals!"

–   "Fight to the last breath!"

Kid (*ready to drop*)**:**

> "P…ple…please! Help them! Eat me but help them.
>
> Help my friends and our parents. Ple…"

Suddenly Kid passed out. Fox and children are seeing a group of wild animals that are coming. One of the Pigeons is showing the way to get the lorry. There is a Pelican among them. Pelican beak is full of water and Goldfish is swimming into that.

An hour later…

Kid took a long time to come round and opened his eyes. A little elephant is pouring water on Kid face. Wolfs, monkeys, bears are chasing Mimi, Titi and other people. Parents are hugging their children. The Leopards and foxes attended wounded animals. The men are escaping towards the city quickly.

<M S> Back of the lorry.

The sounds are heard like making love. These sounds belong to two cats. During the time they were making love in a small box. They were unaware of that much events.

<L S> The great group of animals (wild animals and Pansy animals) thundered surge towards city. They are determined, angry. The sounds of their walks are harmonious and frightening like army boots sounds.

Sequence 36:

EXT.CITY - DAY

< Insert> Loudspeaker, radio, television.

Announcers:

_   **"The vociferous remonstrance of animals of Pansy**

impressed wild animals much."

_   **"Rising of the wild animals for protesting animals**

of Pansy."

_   **"What's the cause of this rising?"**

_   **"According to some reporters…"**

_   **"The cause of this rising…"**

_   **"D.R.A.A didn't fulfill that's promise."**

_   **"Men committed treason against animal."**

_   **"What will be the end of the rising?"**

_   **"Here is peace square in the capital. D.R.A.A."**

_   **"You are watching the animal crowd billow…"**

<L S>The great group of animals are carrying their placards with <Insert>these words on those placards:

_   **"End animal testing."**

- "Make holiday circus!"

- "Stop genocide animal race!"

- "Do you know about the castration results on
  creatures?"

- "No charge animals with Man's silly and disgusting
  acts."

<L S> Animals attacked the zoo and broke jails.

(**Fade in**) (Ambient sound of animal protesters- beating- fighting- boxing- to kick and receive a kick- to shout- to scream- to groan- police's alarm and…)

(**Fade out**) These words in blood on the walls of the city:

<S>

- "Selfish Men have to experience the pain of solitude."

- "They will remove the word "useless" from lexicon
  when they are over exhaust by hard work in the farms
  or to live without meat, milk and egg."

Announcer (man):

"Animals have just left us a week, today. No one
knows where have they gone? There is no trace of
them. They aren't in villages, cities and woods. If
they have left us forever, what destiny will we have
in prospect?"

Announcer (woman):

"Investigations of hidden police show that those
pigeon have set all animals on uproar."

<C U> People's sadly or angrily face. Car accident occurs again and again.

Nervous pedestrians jostle each other and grapple. Children are weeping and they are restless. Pigeons spread many declarations.

<Insert> A declaration.

The declaration statement:

> "This movement will spread in the world quickly."

Announcer scientific news:

> "According news investigation, scientists have found
>
> out that pigeon meat is very useful for health."

Sequence 37:

EXT.PANSY VILLAGE AND CITY - DAY

<LS> Snowy city and Pansy village. It is snowing.

Sequence 38:

INT. PEOPLE'S ROOMS - NIGHT

<S> Sad people that looking at the bowls of soup on the dining tables. Some of them are gazing at their family pictures in last thanksgiving with regret because there were fried turkeys in the middle of the dining tables. Sad Children have stood behind the windows. Some children are looking at the pictures of santa clause and his reindeer in their books and frames on the walls.

The images have adjusted to the narrator's narration.

Narrator:

> "Next New Year won't pleasant and cheerful. There
>
> is neither fried turkey for thanksgiving nor deer
>
> Santa Clause taking gifts children's houses.
>
> It's so much better that you give Santa clause
>
> a gift. Have you ever thought about your gift?
>
> Give thanks to god if your animals have not gone
>
> yet and live with you. Appreciate the worth of
>
> animals and be kind to them. They are creatures

of sensitivity and have remarkable insight especially kindness."

TO BE CONTINUED...

LIDA KORDI